This book is for

_____

With love from

_____

On this date

_____

ZONDERKIDZ

Nighty Night and Good Night
Copyright © 2018 by The MWS Group, LLC
Illustrations © 2018 by The MWS Group, LLC

Illustrated by Tod Carter and painted by Chuck Vollmer

Requests for information should be addressed to:

Zonderkidz, 3900 Sparks Drive SE, Grand Rapids, Michigan 49546

ISBN 978-0-310-76701-5

Design by Diane Mielke

Printed in China

18 19 20 21 22 /DSC / 21 20 19 18 17 16 15 14 13 12 11 10 9 8 7 6 5 4 3 2 1

By GRAMMY® winner
MICHAEL W. SMITH
and MIKE NAWROCKI

Nighty Night
and

Good Night

nurturing
steps™

Every night before he went
to sleep, Ben and his mom
said a simple prayer:

"Dear God,

Thank you for this day.
Please help all of our family
and friends sleep well tonight!

Amen."

But tonight,
Ben wasn't sleepy.

"Uh oh," he thought. "It's time
for bed, but I can't fall asleep."
He switched on his night light.

"Hi, Nighty Nights!"
Ben greeted his fluffy friends.
"Not feeling tired?" asked Lamby.
"Can't go to sleep?" questioned Bear.

"Maybe we can help,"
suggested Sleepy Puppy with a yawn.

"Some people say that counting sheep
helps you fall asleep," said Lamby.

Ben began to count sheep.
"One, two, three, four, five,
six, seven, eight, nine, ten—"

"Um, I only know how to count to ten." Ben frowned.
"Maybe that's not enough sheep for sleep ..."

"Sometimes when I can't sleep, I try
fluffing my pillow," Bear suggested.

Ben tried fluffing his pillow. Fluff, fluff, fluff.

"My pillow is super fluffy," Ben said,
"but I'm still not tired."

"Have you tried yawning?" Sleepy Puppy suggested.
"A few big yawns always makes me sleepy."

Ben stretched his mouth wide and waited for the yawns to come. "Yawn, yawn, yawn ..."

"Well, I'm tired of yawning," Ben said.
"But I'm still not sleepy."

"I suppose there's only one thing left to do," Bear said.

"Yes, it's lullaby time," Sleepy Puppy said.

The Nighty Nights began to play and sing:

"Lay down, sweet child, and go to sleep.
The Lord be with you and give you His peace.
Lay down, sweet child, and go to sleep.
The Lord be with you tonight.

"Lay down, sweet child, and go to sleep.
The Lord be with you and give you His peace.
Lay down, sweet child, and go to sleep.
The Lord be with you tonight."

The lullaby made Ben very sleepy.
"Good night, Ben," Bear said softly.

"I'm getting sleepy too," whispered Sleepy Puppy.

Lamby prayed,

"Dear God, please help Ben
sleep well tonight. Amen."

As Ben drifted off to sleep,
his friends whispered in his ear,
"Nighty night, and good night."

One of the greatest joys of my life is being the parent of five amazing kids and fourteen grandkids. Yes, fourteen. They call me G-Daddy. It is awesome. And what a great responsibility and joy to be able to pour my life into my kids and my grandkids. What a beautiful time in life for our family.

As a grandparent, I have the joy and responsibility to serve our grandkids well. That's why I created Nuturing Steps™—stories and songs that will help shape the faith of our newest generation.

I know you, your children, and grandchildren are going to love Nuturing Steps™. Generations will be blessed by your commitment.

Michael W. Smith

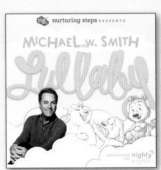

ABOUT **NURTURING STEPS**™

Founded by Michael W. Smith, NURTURING STEPS™ is an infant and toddler series of children's music and books with a simple mission to enliven a little one's journey with hope and faith through music and storytelling.

nurturing steps™

www.nurturingsteps.com